Christmas, Incorporated

A Play in One Act

by Walter Kerr

A SAMUEL FRENCH ACTING EDITION

SAMUEL FRENCH

FOUNDED 1830

SAMUELFRENCH.COM

CHRISTMAS, INCORPORATED

STORY OF THE PLAY

Mary Daly, who works in Connors' Department Store in a large city, remembers the loveliness of her childhood Christmases and the meaning attached to the season. But the feeling she has for Christmas is being savagely destroyed by the gross commercialization of the "seasonal spirit" in the store, and, at the height of the Christmas rush, she decides she can stand it no longer. Another day spent in this brash department - store - manufactured Christmas atmosphere will spoil forever its true significance and, though she is desperately in need of money, she decides to quit. Two of her fellow salesgirls, meeting her in the locker and smoking room of the store, try to dissuade her from carrying out her bitter determination for practical reasons, and she is at the point of giving in when her Connors' Christmas greeting arrives, mangling, for advertising purposes, an old hymn of which she is particularly fond. Angered and ashamed, she takes her coat from the locker to go. A child, waiting for her mother to finish shopping, asks her where she is going. Hoping to prove her point, Mary questions the child about Christmas, feeling that its present shoddy commercialism will have spoiled it for children completely. To her surprise, the child easily explains away the contradiction of sixty seedy Santa Clauses and reveals a feeling for the season very close to Mary's own memory of it. Later, Mary discovers that the child is the daughter of Mr. Connors himself. Finally she goes back to her job, aware now that Christmas is not to be found in the material trappings of a "season," but in one's own heart.

CHRISTMAS, INCORPORATED

CHARACTERS

KAY CARNEY, *a salesgirl.*
EVVIE SMALL, *another.*
MARY DALY, *a salesgirl with a memory.*
MRS. WORRIMAN, *a supervisor.*
LAURA JO, *a child of six.*
LAURA JO'S MOTHER.
PAULINE SIMMS, *a fourth salesgirl.*

THE SCENE: *Interior of the locker and smoking room of Connors' Department Store in a large city.*

THE TIME: *Five days before Christmas. Mid-afternoon.*

CHRISTMAS, INCORPORATED

DESCRIPTION OF CHARACTERS

KAY CARNEY, *a salesgirl in Connors' Department Store. About 24 years old and attractive, but tired. She has accepted most of the things she cannot explain, is practical, sensible in a way that has come through experience rather than intellect, and kindly. She wears a regulation Connors' uniform—black salesdress with white collars and cuffs (detachable).*

EVVIE SMALL, *another salesgirl, wearing the same uniform. She has less understanding than Kay, is more inquisitive and considerably less intelligent. She runs toward the garrulous side, but means well. She is about 10, and substitutes rather apparent makeup for the not too great beauty with which nature has endowed her.*

MARY DALY, *a third salesgirl in the same uniform. But Mary is almost too intelligent for her job. Something of an idealist, she sees beyond the limited range of practical experience of Kay and Evvie to deeper issues. She is an individualist, almost to the point of self-assertiveness, but she has always thought out her moves. If she is emotional, it is because there are good reasons; her sensitivity is a genuine thing. She is about 19 or 20 and attractive even when angry; almost more so when her temper is up, because infuriated determination becomes her pleasantly stubborn face. Her movements are quick, assured, but in an attractive, girlish way.*

MRS. WORRIMAN, *a supervisor in the department store. Her uniform is grey, with cream-colored collar and cuffs. She is domineering, efficient, and practises an affected motherliness and magnanimity which never quite comes off. This "motherliness" is not a sweet one, however; it is rather an advisory, competent, wise one which she feels, with not much justice, is becoming to her position. She is about 48, with dyed hair.*

PAULINE SIMMS, *a fourth salesgirl in regulation uniform. She is about 26, but still excitable and impressionable enough to seem a schoolgirl. She is perhaps a better salesgirl than Kay or Evvie, but it is purely a matter of instinct.*

LAURA JO *is a child of about 6, well-dressed but in a markedly juvenile style. The part, obviously, may be played by an older girl if necessary, but she should be short and rather full-faced. She is cute, alert, inquisitive, and every bit as assertive as Mary with an advantage in the infallible logic of children. She is dressed for outside, in a fur-trimmed child's coat, fur bonnet, muff, and mittens. She also has on a pair of children's galoshes.*

LAURA JO'S MOTHER, *a fashionably-dressed, gracious woman of middle age. Inclined to stoutness, she is still graceful, assured, without being in any way superior in her attitude.*

Christmas, Incorporated

THE SCENE: *Interior of the women's locker room in Connors' Department Store, a major firm in a major city. A row of lockers is seen against the back wall, with wall benches against the Right and Left of the room. A mirror is set into the wall above the benches at Left and a drinking fountain at Right. Several low tables are scattered about the room, with stools near them. A couch Center. There are also several ash trays. This is the room in which Connors' employees adjourn for a hasty cigarette during the day and to which they come at the beginning and ending of working hours for their coats and hats. It is now Christmas time, as we are informed by the presence of a forlorn and rather self-conscious Christmas tree at upstage Right. On it are a number of simple ornaments, linked together with tinseled ribbon which obviously has some sort of a company motto inscribed on it. At the top of the tree is a smiling cardboard face—not Santa Claus, not the Saviour, but Mr. Connors himself. At the base of the tree are two placards, one on each side: "CONNORS GIVES YOU CHRISTMAS" says one; "THE SEASON FOR SMART SHOPPING" says the other. There is an entrance down Left to the store generally. Whenever the door opens we hear the excited buzz of many Christmas shoppers. At present two clerks are on stage, KAY CARNEY and EVVIE SMALL. KAY is at the mirror, applying lipstick; EVVIE is on the short end of a cigarette on bench, Left.*

EVVIE. What'd you do last night, Kay?

KAY. Movie.

EVVIE. What about?

KAY. Love.

EVVIE. Any good?

KAY. Oh, I don't know. When I'm in love, I always like a love picture. And when I ain't, they seem kind of silly.

EVVIE. That's 'cause you're jealous. It's over-composition. I knew a fellow who took psychology once, and that's what he said it was.

KAY. No, it ain't that. I guess I'm just sensitive.

EVVIE. Well, he only took it in night school. Are you in love now?

KAY. Don't ask me. What I want to know is how can anybody be in love this time of year when they're working at Connors'? Love takes a lot of effort, and when you get through a day with those wild women climbing all over the counters out there you ain't got much effort left in you. Johnny—that's the boy I'm going with—he says I ain't got nothing left for him by evening, and he's right, I just ain't, so how do I know if I'm in love?

EVVIE. The season oughta make you feel different. This is the season of love. There was a good cartoon about it in the paper last night. A big city with a lot of noise and traffic and everything, but with the spirit of love flying around on top of it.

KAY. Yeah, I guess I oughta feel that way. What paper was it in? Maybe I'm just out of touch with things, that's all.

(The door suddenly bursts open, admitting for a

split second the raucous SOUND of frantic shoppers, and then is quickly closed by PAULINE SIMMS, *who falls back against it breathlessly.)*

PAULINE. Hey, somebody!

EVVIE. I ain't in here if old horse-face wants me.

PAULINE. It ain't Mrs. Worriman. It's Mary.

KAY. What's the matter with Mary?

PAULINE. One of you'd better go out there and talk to her.

EVVIE. Tell her to come in here.

PAULINE. No, I mean the way she's acting. She's gone off her head. One of the customers—an old dame with fuzzy hair—just asked her why it was that Connors has so much more Christmas spirit than the other stores, and you know what Mary told her?

KAY. *(Anxiously)* What?

PAULINE. *(After a breath, impressively)* She said it was because Mr. Connors had a gentleman's agreement with the Lord and that the store was founded on divine revolution or something.

KAY. Revelation.

EVVIE. *(Crosses and sits on table Left Center)* That's a kind of cold cream, isn't it?

PAULINE. Maybe you can talk to her. She's sassing back the customers and everything—and I'm afraid Mrs. Worriman is gonna hear about it if we don't do something to stop her.

KAY. You can't stop Mary. I wonder what's eating her?

EVVIE. Oh, just because she had a year of college she thinks she's smarter'n other people. She's just showing off.

KAY. No. Mary ain't like that. She's always serious, no matter what.

EVVIE. Well, actin' like that ain't gonna get her back to school, that's certain. She'll just talk herself out of a job and all that money she's been gonna save up for it.

PAULINE. Well, gee! Ain't you gonna do something about it?

KAY. You know, it's funny. Mary used to be real pleasant when she first came here.

EVVIE. Yeah. She even used to say good morning to Mrs. Worriman.

KAY. You know, maybe we *had* better—

PAULINE. Well, that's up to you. I've done all I could. I've gotta get back on the floor right away or maybe I won't get tonight off.

(She turns and opens the door as though to go; just as she does, MARY comes into the room, furious. With an obvious attempt at restraining rage, she crosses the room rapidly and stands tensely before the Christmas tree, glaring at it. The three GIRLS watch her curiously, then PAULINE gives them an "I told you so!" nod and goes, closing the door behind her. After a moment, the other two GIRLS venture to break the strained silence with casual conversation, keeping their eyes on the silently furious MARY.)

EVVIE. Huh! She talks about nights off. I ain't had a night off in two weeks on account of that extra time off when I was sick. I worked till nine-thirty last night and then we had to stay late and check things for this morning. I thought my feet would go crazy.

KAY. Anyway, it's only five more days. Then we get nights off again.

EVVIE. With a holiday at Christmas and New Year's!

KAY. But think of inventory. All during January!

Evvie. Oh, Lord! And the stuff those dames bring back.

(Then Mary, *who apparently has heard nothing outside her own raging head, suddenly lets one foot fly and kicks over the placard reading "THE SEASON FOR SMART SHOP- PING." Without turning, she goes to the bench at Right and sits on it, swinging her feet up with her. She crosses her arms over her knees and stares furiously into space.)*

Kay. What do you suppose has got into our Mary?

Evvie. Used to have such a nice disposition, too. Mr. Connors smiled at her once on account of it.

Mary. *(Without looking up at them)* Shut up!

Evvie. It ain't the same old Mary, I can see that.

Mary. You can't see anything.

Evvie. *(With a tolerant glance at* Kay*)* Well, my doctor says I need glasses, but I guess I'll wait and get married first and then get glasses. I figure you ain't got much of a chance if you look too sensible. Guys always say they want every part of you, but I guess that don't include technical improvements. *(After a pause)* What's eating you, Mary? *(But they are met with a rigid silence.)*

Kay. She's in a mood, that's all. Leave her alone. I get moods, too.

Evvie. She's anti-social, that's what that psychologist I knew used to call it.

Kay. I thought he just took a course.

Evvie. He auditioned it. I guess that's different. You get to know more.

Mary. *(Savagely, still staring front)* Hell!

Kay. Somebody must of bit her.

Evvie. Maybe a customer. Personally, the **next**

time one of 'em does, I'm gonna bite right back. My eyes ain't so good, but my teeth are all right.

MARY. So are mine. If you don't shut up, you'll find out.

KAY. You don't have to talk like an animal.

EVVIE. We all got animal instincts. It's heresy, or something. Only you shouldn't let 'em go like that, Mary.

KAY. It ain't like you, Mary.

EVVIE. No, it ain't. You're usually so nice, and now, at Christmas time, when *everybody's* nice—

MARY. Are they?

KAY. Oh, oh! Now I see. Somebody rubbed her the wrong way.

MARY. Not somebody. Something.

EVVIE. What?

MARY. Christmas!

KAY *and* EVVIE. *(At once)* Christmas?

MARY. Christmas! Christmas at Connors'!

EVVIE. Well—what's Connors got to do with it?

MARY. Nothing. He only owns it; that's all.

KAY. What does he own?

EVVIE. The store? Well, I should hope.

MARY. No, not the store, stupids! Christmas!

EVVIE. *(After an utterly perplexed pause)* Well, I knew my eyes were bad, but I guess there must be something the matter with the rest of my head or else that just doesn't make any sense.

MARY. He's got a monopoly on it.

KAY. On Christmas?

MARY. Now you're getting somewhere.

EVVIE. Well, *I'm* in the same old place. It's a mystery to me.

MARY. It should be a mystery to everybody.

EVVIE. *(Almost in despair) What* should?

MARY. Christmas! Only it isn't.

EVVIE. A mystery? You mean like "Murder On

Christmas Eve" or "Who Killed Santa Claus" or something?

MARY. No, I don't. But I know who did kill Santa Claus. I've seen the murder.

EVVIE. Maybe you'll get your picture in the paper. A guy I knew was a witness once. Only that was a real murder. *(With sudden exasperation)* Honest, Mary, I don't know what you're talking about, and it ain't often I admit that.

KAY. I know what she means. It ain't a mystery with murders and blood and clues and that stuff. It's the other kind of a mystery—*you* know—mysterious. Something you believe but you can't explain.

EVVIE. Oh! I never thought of Christmas that way. I don't think I could exactly explain it, though. You just work nights for a month ahead of it, then you get a day off, and then you take inventory, but you feel good. It's funny you should feel good with all that work in back of you and all that work ahead of you, but you do, don't you? I guess that's mysterious.

KAY. Well—maybe! I don't think I could explain Christmas either.

MARY. I can.

EVVIE. Well, what is it, then?

MARY. It's a national fire-sale.

EVVIE. Oh, my goodness!

KAY. That's kind of indecent, Mary.

MARY. That's what it is, though. Christmas is indecent—now.

EVVIE. Christmas is sacred, Mary. That's what my mother always said, and she knew about stuff like that. She was sort of holy, I guess. At least that's what Dad said after he started drinking.

MARY. Your father worked for Connors, didn't he?

Evvie. *(With a trace of pride)* Yes. My father before me.

Mary. No wonder he started drinking. He was ahead of his time.

Kay. What have you got against Connors, anyway?

Evvie. Besides the meals in the lunchroom?

Kay. How could Connors have a monopoly on Christmas? That's just plain silly. Christmas belongs to everybody.

Mary. But they have to go to the department stores to get it.

Evvie. *(A great dawn has broken)* Oh, you mean the presents.

Mary. I mean the presents and the tinsel and the trees and the holly and the feeling and the spirit and the whole sensation of Christmas. That's what I mean.

Evvie. That's a large order. I hope I don't have to take it.

Mary. Christmas is lived in the department stores.

Kay. That sounds like a quotation.

Mary. Christmas *is* a quotation. But a financial one. In six figures for Connors, and sixty for all the other department stores in the country. And I'm sick of it.

Kay. It helps pay your salary.

Mary. Exactly! The first duty of Christmas is to pay salaries. *And* dividends! God on a paying basis. Bah!

Evvie. *(Rising angrily)* Mary, you're just getting plain vulgar, and I won't listen to it, that's all! I just won't.

Mary. All right, don't! By all means, don't listen to anything vulgar. You go right back out there into the store and get an earful of something dignified and beautiful. That's what we've got—the dignity and beauty of Christmas! The store reeks with it.

All you have to do is go out there and let your soul absorb it, let it inspire you, let yourself wallow in the sacred spirit of Connors. Go ahead, I don't care.

EVVIE. *(Taken aback)* Well, you don't have to get so excited.

MARY. Oh, don't I! Don't I, though? Why shouldn't I get excited? When I was a little girl I used to get excited about Christmas—why shouldn't I now? I have to get excited about it in a different way, of course. I used to want to see Santa Claus. Well, now all I can see is Santa Clauses—sixty of 'em, one in every department! I used to pray for snow—lots of it, heaps of it! But Connors doesn't want snow—it keeps people in their unChristmasy little houses and out of the big festive department stores. I used to like to sing songs about jingling bells, especially when it got to be night time. Now I get bells all day—a chorus of 'em, from the elevators and the store phones and the special demonstrators who show you how to fill stockings with Connors candies, and the only thing that jingles is the cash registers. Children used to lie on the floor and read illustrated picture books about a Child born in a manger. Now they read the latest advertisements from Connors, filled with colors and cartoons, and the only connection between the two is that the stuff we advertise is mangy.

KAY. Don't let Mrs. Worriman hear you say that.

MARY. I don't care who hears me. I want to be heard. I feel just like a Connors loud speaker or a Connors radio program, and I want to do some commercial plugging. I want to plug up Connors' grinning map, for one thing. We used to have an angel on top of *our* Christmas tree—not that thing! *(She points furiously to the grinning mask of Connors atop the tree.)* But Connors has taken over Christmas, and I guess the wings went with it. *(Looking at the remaining placard beneath the tree and read-*

ing it) "CONNORS GIVES YOU CHRISTMAS."
(With a quick thrust of her foot, she kicks it over, too) Connors gives *me* a pain in the neck.

EVVIE. *(Sympathetically)* You ain't got no delusions left, have you?

MARY. *(Slumping onto the bench again, despondently, her wrath over)* Sixty seedy Santa Clauses! My God, what do children think? If I had a kid, I'd tell her. I'd tell her the way things *are*.

KAY. Oh, you ain't a child any more. What do you care?

MARY. *(Quietly, almost tearfully)* I care because there isn't any Christmas any more. It's just a paying institution.

EVVIE. You been working too hard, dearie.

MARY. I've been working hard trying to feel— like I used to feel this time of year. And it won't come back. It won't come back because all I can hear is my own nasty little voice saying *(in a saleslady's voice)* "Merry Christmas from Connors. Connors Gives You Christmas." I even hate myself.

KAY. Well, you've made your big speech. Now you can go back and start saying those other things again.

MARY. No.

EVVIE. What?

MARY. I won't go back. I won't go back out there.

KAY. Don't be silly. Mrs. Worriman is gonna miss you in a couple of minutes.

MARY. Mrs. Worriman is going to miss me the rest of her days.

EVVIE. *(Aghast)* You don't mean you'd quit?

MARY. Connors has made Christmas quit on me. So I'm quitting on Connors.

EVVIE. Oh! Oh—that's terrible!

MARY. Why?

EVVIE. Why, I mean—just before Christmas.

MARY. That's why I'm quitting. In five days it'll

be Christmas, and when it's here I want to feel like Christmas. If I stay in this place, it'll die inside me just like it did last year.

KAY. I'd think it over, Mary. You need the money awful bad. You've been outa school two years now, and if you're ever gonna get back—

EVVIE. Yeah! That's what you want most, ain't it?

MARY. I did. But what good'll it do me to learn how to live life, if the life I have to live has been spoiled? Right now Christmas is more important. And what good's a lovely thing like Christmas if you wear it out at Connors? If it isn't in your heart, why have it? I'm going to get my dirty black coat out of that locker over there and slam it behind me for the last time.

EVVIE. I thought—you were getting a *new* coat. That black one's kind of—well, mangy. That's the word you said.

MARY. I was going to do that, too. For Christmas. But you can get the feeling of a new coat any time. It won't make up for Christmas.

KAY. *(Lights cigarette)* It won't feel much like Christmas—in that old coat.

MARY. Sure! There's the whole department-store Christmas in a nutshell! You think as long as you've got a new package with a green and red ribbon saying "Christmas Time is Connors' Time" tied around it, you've got the spirit of the thing, too. You and all those snarling people out there.

KAY. They seem to get some—happiness out of it, though. Even if it's wrapped up in a box from Connors'.

MARY. That's because they're blind. They can't see through the silly things they do. *(A pause)* I did want that coat.

KAY. Sure you did.

EVVIE. Mrs. Worriman would give you a discount if you bought it here.

MARY. All my life comes through Connors. When I die, they'll wrap my coffin in cellophane and stamp it "COURTESY OF CONNORS." I won't have it. I won't.

EVVIE. It won't be much like Christmas to be out of work.

KAY. And you thought next year you might be in school—

MARY. Oh— *(She turns away from them with a shrug of her shoulders.)*

EVVIE. I was out of work one Christmas, the same time as my sister was. That was before she got married. It wasn't—much fun. We didn't dare spend anything 'cause we didn't know when we'd get work again, and my sister, she couldn't get married because Mom didn't have any money put aside to take care of herself in case I didn't get work. We had a special dinner, of course, but it seemed sort of flat without any tree or any boxes or candy and stuff. And then—maybe it was because we didn't send any cards, I don't know—but nobody stopped in to say "Merry Christmas" that day, and—it wasn't much fun.

KAY. *(After a pause)* I'd think it over, Mary. Honest I would.

MARY. *(Weakening)* Oh, well—

EVVIE. *(Crossing to MARY and kissing her on the cheek)* It's just like Kay says, honey, it's just a mood. You'll get over it. I'll tell the old horse you'll be on the counter again in a minute. *(As EVVIE crosses toward the door at Left, it opens and MRS. WORRIMAN comes in briskly. She is the department supervisor, with an authoritative manner, and she carries a large stack of envelopes on her arm.)*

EVVIE. Oh, hello, Mrs. Worriman! We were just speaking of you.

MRS. WORRIMAN. Mr. Connors does not approve

of inter-departmental gossip, Miss Small. Haven't you girls been in here rather long?

Evvie. It's my feet, Mrs. Worriman. I was on duty last night again.

Mrs. Worriman. It was your feet last night, too, as I remember.

Evvie. Well, I was just going back now—

Mrs. Worriman. Well, you may take this with you. *(She hands her one of the envelopes)* It won't help your feet any, but it may perhaps show you that Mr. Connors is always thinking of his employees.

Evvie. Thank you, Mrs. Worriman! I'm sure he is. (Evvie *goes into the store, admitting the HUB-BUB for a moment, then closing the door behind her.)*

Mrs. Worriman. *(Staring at* Kay*) You* weren't on duty last night, Miss Carney.

Kay. *(Keeping one hand behind her back)* I— may I finish my cigarette, Mrs. Worriman?

Mrs. Worriman. *(Giving her an envelope)* With the compliments of Connors. Yes, but be sure you place the stub in an ashtray, *not* on the Connors floor! (Mrs. Worriman *turns and crosses to* Mary, *giving her envelope)* And one for you, young lady. You needn't look so very unpleasant, either. I've been hearing funny things about you. The customers expect Connors employees to exude the seasonal spirit, and I don't want to have to call this to your attention again.

(Meanwhile Kay *has hastily moved her hand from behind her back, revealing in it the very short stub of a cigarette. Deftly, she fishes another cigarette out of her package on the bench and lights it from the stub. She grinds the stub into the floor with her heel, keeping an eye on* Mrs. Worriman's *back as she talks with* Mary, *and*

then scuffs the stub under the bench. At the same time, with her other hand, she has hurriedly slipped back the flap of the envelope and glanced at its contents.)

MARY. I—I guess I'm sorry, Mrs. Worriman.

MRS. WORRIMAN. You *guess?*

KAY. *(Interrupting quickly)* Oh, I think it's an awfully nice Christmas card, Mrs. Worriman. I think it's just awfully nice.

MRS. WORRIMAN. *(Crossing toward the door at Left again)* I'm glad you do. Mr. Connors chose to distribute them this way this year. Don't be too long about that cigarette. And do brighten up, Miss Daly. *(Adjusting the envelopes)* I think it was very thoughtful of Mr. Connors myself. It's so much more personal. *(She goes into the store, closing the door behind her.)*

MARY. And saves postage.

(MRS. WORRIMAN *quickly thrusts open the door again, popping her head into the room as though she had heard the remark. She stares at them a moment before speaking.)*

MRS. WORRIMAN. And remember the floors. *(Then she is gone again.* KAY *rises and stretches herself.)*

KAY. I almost didn't get this lit fast enough. Want one?

MARY. Oh—I guess so. Might as well before I—go back out there. (MARY *takes one and* KAY *lights it for her.)*

KAY. I'm glad you're going back.

MARY. I'm not. *(Opening the envelope)* But who am I to want what no one else seems to get any more?

KAY. They get a kick out of it out there, Mary. Honest they do.

MARY. It's so manufactured, that's all. It's— *(She has glanced at the envelope; she lets a sharp, explosive gasp escape her.)*

KAY. Huh? You say something?

MARY. *(After a stupefied pause)* Kay—you remember, I was telling you about when I was a little girl. And about Christmas?

KAY. Sure. Sure. What is it?

MARY. We used to sing songs in the evening. One of them—one of them was called "Hark! The Herald Angels Sing."

KAY. I heard that. Just last night, at the movie. They played it while the management wished us a Merry Christmas and announced next year's pictures.

MARY. This—this card—

KAY. What is it? You ain't fired or something?

MARY. No. It's just the Christmas card. *(Bitterly)* That's all.

KAY. Well—mine was all right.

MARY. *(Furiously)* Was it?

KAY. Why, what's the matter?

MARY. *(Rising angrily)* Let me read it to you. Let me read it out loud so I can hear it ring in my ears like a quaint old carol. It says: *(And* KAY *looks curiously at her own while* MARY *reads, unable to discover* MARY's *objection.)*

> "Hark! the herald angels sing,
>   As they gifts from Connors bring;
>   Peace on earth, prosperity,
>   Connors works for you and me!
>   Joyful all ye nations rise
>   To discover Connors' ties,
>   Shirts, and lingerie galore
>   From our bargain basement store!
>   Hark the herald angels sing,
>   'Connors first in everything!' "

(MARY *stares almost speechless at the card. Then she tries to read it again, almost unbelieving—)* "Hark! the herald angels sing,
    As they gifts from Conn—" *(But her voice fades into nothingness. Her mouth becomes set.)*
KAY. *(Bewildered)* Well, gee, Mary—
MARY. That settles it. Once and for all!
KAY. Oh, Mary, don't—

(The door opens and MRS. WORRIMAN *appears rather tentatively. She bustles a nicely dressed* CHILD *of about six years in ahead of her.)*

MRS. WORRIMAN. I want one of you girls to take care of Laura Jo for a few moments, do you hear? Her mother will be in shortly. Mary—you'd better do it. The department feels that Miss Carney has consumed sufficient cigarettes for a battalion today. Miss Carney, on your counter, please. (KAY *goes quickly to the door, almost throwing the cigarette to the floor, then remembering and stopping long enough to douse it in an ashtray.)* Laura Jo, now, you run over there to Miss Daly. She'll take care of you.

*(*MARY *has neither turned to her nor answered, but* MRS. WORRIMAN *waits for no one. She lets* KAY *go into the store before her, then follows, closing the door, leaving* LAURA Jo *staring in a puzzled fashion at the immobile* MARY.*)*

LAURA Jo. Hullo!
MARY. *(Suddenly coming to life, savagely)* Goodbye! *(She crosses swiftly to the locker, opens it, and takes out her coat.)*
LAURA Jo. Aren't you going to stay with me?
MARY. No. *(She is hastily removing the cuffs from her sleeves.)*

LAURA JO. Why not?

MARY. Because I'm going away and never coming back.

LAURA JO. Not ever?

MARY. Not even then.

LAURA JO. My mother's gone to see somebody. Are you going to see somebody?

MARY. I'm going to see if I can find—somebody.

LAURA JO. Who?

MARY. Christmas.

LAURA JO. Christmas isn't a person, it's a day. *(She giggles)* You thought it was a person because its first name is Mary, didn't you?

MARY. No. *My* first name is Mary, and that's an old joke besides. I'm just running away from a new joke, that's all.

LAURA JO. You're not really going to find somebody. You're just pretending.

MARY. Can't I convince *anybody* today? *(She throws her cuffs to the floor)* Sure I'm going to find somebody. I'm going to find Santa Claus.

LAURA JO. Oh, that's easy. I just saw him. You don't have to put on your coat. He's right here in this store. Haven't you seen him?

MARY. Sure! Sixty of him!

LAURA JO. *(Giggling again)* You're awful silly. Those are his helpers.

MARY. His what?

LAURA JO. His helpers. He's got so very much work to do, he has to have some helpers. Just like in a battle—my brother Billy, his real name is William, but everybody calls him Billy except my mother— he's got lots of soldiers and they all look alike, but only one is the General and all the rest are helpers.

MARY. *(Looking at her steadily for the first time, catching a bit of the contagious and terrible rationality of children)* But the General has a medal or something that makes him different.

Laura Jo. Well—Santa Claus, the real one, has more whiskers. I kissed him and some came off on me.

Mary. You didn't make the rounds, I don't suppose?

Laura Jo. What?

Mary. You didn't kiss them all? The helpers, I mean.

Laura Jo. Oh, no! Mother says as long as I kiss the important one, he'll take care of everything for me. He's the one that has the reindeer. The others just load the sleigh, that's all. It's the one with the reindeer that brings the presents.

Mary. *(Curiously)* And the presents—do they ever have a name written on them? Besides Santa Claus?

Laura Jo. Oh, yes! Sometimes they have mine, too.

Mary. *(Cautiously)* And why—why do you suppose all those people out there—in the store—come here and look at all these pres—these pretty things, then?

Laura Jo. Well, goodness me! You're just silly. How can my mother tell what presents to ask for if she doesn't look at the stores and see what kind of things Santa Claus can get for me?

Mary. Doesn't—Santa Claus make his own presents?

Laura Jo. Oh, yes, but how can he keep up with the stores if he doesn't know what they make? I suppose if he didn't make as good presents as the kind people can buy, nobody would want his, would they?

Mary. You—you know all the answers, don't you?

Laura Jo. My mother says she just can't wait till I go to school.

MARY. *(Definitely interested)* Tell me—do you know any Christmas songs?

LAURA Jo. Oh, sure! Lots! My father, he's so stupid, he doesn't know any any more, but my grandma teaches me lots. Sometimes Granny and I sing "Jingle Bells" and sometimes we sing one about Bethlehem.

MARY. Do you know one called—"Hark! The Herald Angels Sing"?

LAURA Jo. No—I don't think so. But it sounds nice. I'll ask Granny to teach me. She knows "Silent Night," though. She knows it in German, too, only I can't tell it except by the tune when she sings it that way.

MARY. And—does your granny like Christmas so very, very much, too?

LAURA Jo. Oh, yes! She loves it. One time she said she didn't used to like it, for a while anyhow, but now she says she likes it again. I don't know why.

MARY. *(Is silent for a moment)* Tell your granny I love her.

LAURA Jo. You don't even know her. You're awful silly. I like you, but you're awful silly. Shall I kiss you?

MARY. Being kissed is a feeling—like Christmas. (LAURA Jo *gets onto the bench and kisses* MARY.)

LAURA Jo. There! It's better without whiskers. (MARY *laughs, her eyes a trifle wet. But before she can say anything further, the door opens and* EVVIE *comes in with* LAURA Jo's MOTHER.)

EVVIE. Oh, yes, ma'am, she's right in here, Mrs. Worriman said. Sure enough! Have you and Mary been talking about things, Laura Jo?

LAURA Jo. We've been talking about Christmas.

EVVIE. *(Suddenly dismayed)* Oh, my goodness!

LAURA Jo's MOTHER. She's talked of nothing else

for months. You know how exciting and romantic it is for the children.

LAURA JO. I told her about Granny, Mum. She says she likes Granny.

LAURA JO'S MOTHER. That's kind of her, isn't it, darling? *(Turning to* MARY*)* Thank you for being so agreeable, Miss— *(But* MARY *is lost in speculation.* EVVIE *jumps into the gap.)*

EVVIE. Lane. Mary Lane, that's her name.

MARY. *(Awakening to the situation)* Yes. And— I've enjoyed knowing Laura Jo. She's a bright child. She'll do well in school, I think.

LAURA JO'S MOTHER. We can't wait to get her started. We have high hopes for Laura Jo—both Mr. Connors and myself.

MARY. *(Eyes wide)* Mr.——?

LAURA JO'S MOTHER. Thank you again, both of you. Come, dear! *(She takes* LAURA JO'S *hand at the door.)*

LAURA JO. Goodbye!

EVVIE. Goodbye, Laura Jo! Good afternoon, Mrs. Connors.

(LAURA JO *and her mother,* MRS. CONNORS, *go out.* EVVIE *closes the door after them; turns to* MARY, *who has been standing with her mouth open.)*

EVVIE. Well, what are you gaping at?

MARY. Mrs.—?

EVVIE. Mrs. Connors. You've heard of her. Connors' Department Store, remember?

MARY. *(Falling into a chair)* My stars! My blessed, blessed stars! *(And she begins to laugh, lightly.)* *(WARN Curtain.)*

EVVIE. Your moods are awful alternative today.

MARY. *(Half-consciously putting her cuffs back on again)* She said the presents sometimes had her name on them, but I never—

Evvie. Well, if I was curious, I'd probably want to know what you're talking about, but your explanations only leave me worse off than ever, and I never *do* see what—

Mary. *(A bit dazedly)* I guess seeing depends on your eyes. Hang up my coat, will you?

Evvie. You helpless?

Mary. *(Opening the door to the store)* More or less. I guess I need—a helper. *(She goes into the store.)*

(Evvie looks after her curiously a moment, then starts down to the door, too. As she reaches it, Pauline comes in again.)

Pauline. *(Crossing to the drinking fountain)* My Lord! You in here again? You just came out of here, I thought.

Evvie. *(At the doorway, looking into the store)* Huh? Oh, no! It was an hour, anyway.

Pauline. *(Sitting on the bench at Right and taking out a cigarette)* You know, I been thinking. Did it ever strike you that all this Christmas setup is kind of cheap and fakey?

(But Evvie is listening to something else. Through the doorway and amid the hubbub of the shoppers, we hear Mary's pleasant voice: "Merry Christmas from Connors, ma'am. What did you wish? Thank you so much. Connors gives you Christmas." Evvie closes the door slowly.)

Pauline. I said did it ever strike you that all this Christmas setup is kind of cheap and fakey?

Evvie. *(Vaguely)* Why, no—not that I know of. I don't think it ever did. Gee, my feet are killing me!

CURTAIN

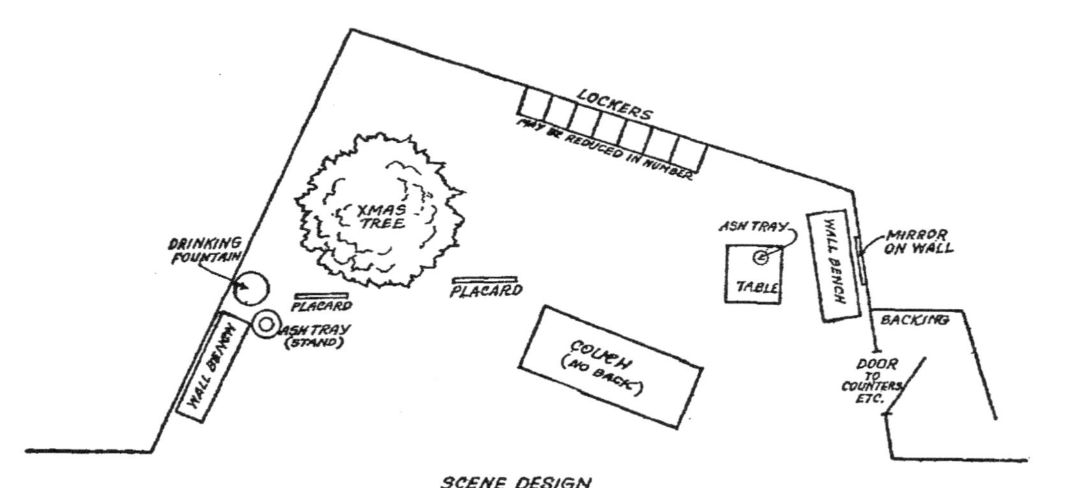

SCENE DESIGN
"CHRISTMAS, INC."